For my Ruby, who really did love pinecones – SCN

For T.J. and Alban – EFC

ISBN: 9781794304826

Summary: A dog named Ruby discovers that pinecones not only make the perfect playthings, but they make her feel brave as well.

Ruby
and the
Pinecones

Susan C Nikiel

Illustrations by Emma Fern Curtis

Ruby lived with her family in a doggy paradise where she could run free, play hard, and sniff, sniff, sniff all day long.

She was much like any other Golden Retriever pup – a tail-wagging, ball-fetching, dirt-digging bundle of energy and happiness.

Her whole body wiggled when she wagged her tail and her eyes seemed to dance when she was happy.

Ruby especially liked belly rubs, walks in the woods, and rolling in the mud when she wanted to pretend to be a Chocolate Lab.

Ruby woke one morning to a hot summer day and set out to explore her great, big world.

She felt much like she did on any other day – curious and playful, but also a bit like a scaredy pup. She was frightened of frogs, uncertain around umbrellas, and nervous about noises.

She wondered what the day would bring. "Squirrels to chase? Stinky smells to roll in? Scary stuff?"

Brother and Sister were outside inventing new games to play.

Ruby followed along as she often did, watching as Brother and Sister threw rocks into the river, built a fort out of branches, and collected pinecones – large, prickly pinecones!

Ruby heard a new sound with her keen doggy ears. *Bang! Rattle, rattle! Thud!*

She heard it again! This time, Brother and Sister's laughter joined the new experience.

"What was that?" wondered Ruby as she looked toward the sound. Curious, Ruby tilted her head.

Then she saw it! Pinecones were falling from the sky. *Thud!* They would hit the ground.

The pinecones that had before laid still on the ground came alive with new possibilities!

Brother and Sister were throwing pinecones on to the metal roof of the garage. Curious, and a little frightened, Ruby watched the new game.

Ruby followed the sound of the bang, rattle, rattle. Then she saw the pinecone reach the edge of the roof and launch into the air.

"Flying pinecone", Ruby thought, "will it get me? Will it hurt me?" *Thud!* The pinecone hit the ground and stayed where it had landed.

The curious part of Ruby sniffed and nudged the pinecone with her nose while the scaredy part was ready to run away.

She picked the pinecone up with her mouth and gave it a squeeze. *Crunch!!*

"Nothing to be afraid of, only fun
found here", she said.

Ruby noticed just how many pinecones
lay on the ground and now wished that they
would all come sailing off of the roof.

The next pinecone that rattled
on the roof made Ruby feel excited!

She couldn't wait for it to land
on the ground, so she leaped up and
caught it in mid-air.

Ruby stood there, pinecone in mouth,
tail wagging, feeling brave, and looked at
Mother expectantly.

Ruby let Mother have the pinecone, who then threw it across the yard where it skittered along the ground.

Without even thinking, Ruby raced after the pinecone. She couldn't help herself as she was a fetcher and the new toy needed fetching!

She snatched it up in her mouth and ran back to Mother. Ruby dropped the pinecone at Mother's feet. *Plop!*

"Pinecone, pinecone. Fetch, fetch, fetch!" Ruby's sparkling eyes seemed to say.

Because fetching was fun and pinecones were the perfect plaything, this game now became the best game. Her eyes sparkled brighter, her tail wagged faster, and her feet danced!

Never had Ruby been happier! Now that she had experienced the pleasure of pinecones Ruby felt more than energetic.

"I feel practically **PIZAZZY**!" she said.

Ruby kept pinecones with her all day long. She would try to carry as many as her mouth would hold and she looked so funny with her wide, pineconey grin.

She encouraged Father to be a fetch-player and loved that he could throw SO far!

He threw pinecones for her until she was tuckered out, with her tongue loose and hanging, and panting with contentment.

Pinecones, Ruby had discovered, made great toys, but she also found that they made her feel deliriously happy, daringly brave, and never alone.

When with a mouthful of pinecones Ruby found frogs less frightening. In fact, Ruby would now go to the pond to see if the frog wanted to play with her.

As for umbrellas...not nearly so unsettling. Knowing that pinecones were near made noises seem like nothing.

Pinecones made Ruby feel brave, even around a noisy frog with an umbrella!

Ruby finally understood how Sister felt about her blankie and Brother about his stuffed toy monkey.

It was wonderful to have something special of her own that made her life feel even better.

As evening came and she was inside snoozing by the fire, Ruby was dreaming about her day of discovery and the pleasures of pinecones.

Even in her sleep her paws wiggled and her ears twitched. Ruby seemed to be smiling!

"Pinecone, pinecone, fetch, fetch, fetch!"

Made in the USA
San Bernardino, CA
23 April 2019